what's that
size?

Kate Petty and
Lisa Kopper

Franklin Watts
New York · London · Toronto · Sydney

Jack has never been
to the zoo before.
Amy is going
to show him
all the animals.

DATE		
NOV 05 1987	AUG 06 1991	JUL 29 1994
NOV 25 1987	AUG 22 1991	APR 08 1997
	SEP 05 1991	MAY 22 1997
DEC 10 1987	OCT 15 1991	JUL 25 1997
FEB 04 1988	OCT 29 1991	DEC 23 1997
APR 08 1988		JAN 09 1998
APR 21 1988	DEC 03 1991	JAN 16 1998
JUN 16 1988	OCT 14 1992	
FEB 15 1991	OCT 15 1993	

Published in the United States in 1987 by
Franklin Watts, 387 Park Avenue South, New York, NY10016

© Aladdin Books Ltd

Designed and produced by
Aladdin Books Ltd, 70 Old Compton Street, London W1

ISBN 0-531-10282-3
Library of Congress
Catalog Card No 86-50742

Printed in Belgium

Look at the elephant, Jack.
It's so **big**!

Amy and Sarah
run on ahead.

What can they
be looking at
up there?

They are watching the giraffes.
Giraffes are very *tall*.

The hippos will make Jack laugh.
Where are they?
Sarah has seen them.

The hippos walk slowly
out of the water.
They do look *fat*.

These birds like the water too.
Amy and Sarah pretend to be pink flamingoes.

They are all standing
on one leg.

Flamingoes have two legs really.
Their legs are **thin**, like sticks.

Jack is glad the snakes are behind glass.
Here's a python.

Watch it uncoil.
Isn't it **long**!

Dad checks his watch.
Soon it will be
feeding time for
the sea lions.

Everybody wants to see.
Amy and Sarah
can push to the front.

Jack can't see anything.
He's too **short**.
Dad lifts him up.

Now Jack has
the best view of all.

There are no fierce animals
in the children's corner.

They stroke the rabbits
and the guinea pigs.

One of them has babies.
They're so *small!*

The children are thirsty.
Sarah's dad buys everyone a drink.

The wasps like the drinks
but Amy doesn't like the wasps,
even though they're **tiny**.

Buzz off, wasps.

Jack loves the baby chimpanzees.
He could watch them forever.

They are just the
same size as he is.

Say goodbye now, Jack.
It's time to go home.

tall

fat

big

thin

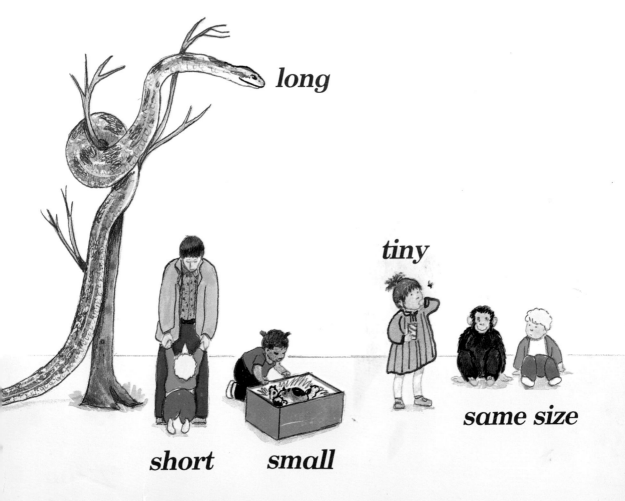

long

tiny

short   small   same size